A *Beginning* AFTER THE *End*

JOHN HENRY DAM

A BEGINNING AFTER THE END
Copyright © 2022 John Henry Dam

Media Literary Excellence
508 West 26th Street, Kearney, NE 68848
www.medialiteraryexcellence.com
1-402-819-3224

ISBN (Paperback): 978-1-958082-06-5
ISBN (Ebook): 978-1-958082-07-2

Printed in the United States of America

Chapter One

AN ODDITY IT SEEMED, BUT it was stark reality, and nothing more than just that. A state representing in itself as being finished! Or was this an aberration that would simply justify what may be a pipe dream? Time would tell as in all things and in due course whichever the case was or wasn't, Rudy had to face the certainty that all ordeals of the past had taken a toll on him. What a calamity and the forbidden reality of its finish-definite or unsure-it-was-over, or seemed to be so. That which paved way for a coveted conclusion was months of mental debilitation, it being a post situation that added to the plaguing confusion.

Attention, Rudy's, which enhances awareness was less than normal and for that reason a slight consciousness loomed in the sleepy outskirts of his oh-so-weary mind. This, which had become usual, was an experience that occurred most prevalent when awakening. What Rudy was trying to articulate was the powerlessness of accepting the truth and that a nightmare of infidelity had come to pass-as it should-for what was done was done. A choice to - or not to - have trouble accepting this was not an option to a desirable end but quite the opposite. There was, to a great extent, a longing, a longing for closing stages to this drawn-out ordeal. The menacing anguish, a torment referring to the insanity which was massive that stemmed from the madness perpetuated while anticipating the lunacy to be gone. Ludicrous it may seem, but he was not overly sure that a desirable closing stage had or would ever come about. "How could she?" A question posed and the answer being evasive, lying in wait, secreted.

Carrying on in this fashion while speculating out loud, he was making a stab at thinking logically, for his thoughts were of a shocking case of death and infidelity. Her actions -self-centered - were out of place; moreover, they brought about an end product of enormous destruction. Unfortunately, Rudy truly was the key recipient of the unwelcomed heartache.

This in mind, it is essential to point out Rudy had done not one thing except work the proverbial tail to the bone. This mode of existence resulting upon the reception of but not deserving many, or actually not even one of the various out of place costs.

Her fleeting gratification was the extreme that nearly ushered him over the edge where a point of no return lie in wait. Luckily, Rudy had a grip on reality and did not collapse, although nearly, but fortunately even though elusive as it may have been managing to maintain his wherewithal was a triumph in itself. If not having managed keeping his wits it was a guarantee that plunging to his demise would be the account resulting from an orchestrated doom that would have resulted in death. The reward assuredly would have been notoriety in the local gazette. Subsequently, the next claim to fame would have been front page headlines. Twenty-four hours of acknowledgement, an infamy ploy that he was in no hurry to claim. Just plain and simple, this man, to whom people would have paid respects, then closely following these fine people would have forgotten he had even existed. Then as a result, would have inquired the oncoming week, what was old what's his name doing when he bit the dirt? You know who I'm trying to remember. Darn it, you know! That cowboy sort of a guy.

Then there was a death, the death of his son. It was a death harvesting the very center of his soul. The toll on him was huge, yes, very much so. While wishing for the haunting memory of his cherished offspring to vanish from daily thought, Rudy then would attempt to submerge these uncontrolled remembrances in the depths of the subconscious and beyond. The loss whether it be referred to as his, hers or theirs would be honored on Decoration Day and is mandatory ... needless to say.

Decoration Day, as it was called a time ago but presently christened Memorial Day, a day that is special. This is a time set aside to remember and honor those whom are loved yet physically are no longer accounted for. Intentionally for that reason he will never be far from mind although a bodily void will be in the balance.

Obtaining his bearings was a feat in itself, a very difficult feat and quite complex to say the least. Rudy simply hated these stupors of indecision that nearly always induced an in significant amount of panic, which at the time didn't seem so insignificant. Then, rubbing his peepers while at the same time putting forth an adequate amount of effort to gain composure and wondering how long he had slept. It made not the slightest of differences, although dealing with post insurmountable chaos it seemed he had just retired. Yet pointing out, if this was the case, he questions how he was able to have a depiction of the undesirable events in such a pictorial chronological order and so vividly? He, nearly overwhelmed, was not able to grasp the situation of time in hand. Trying not to be flustered, Rudy lay back, relaxed and closed his eyes. His plan was doing this momentarily – object attempting a mind adjustment.

The reality of an unwelcome grief was at its life's end. The complexity of accepting this was factual yet extremely difficult, for times clock had ticked to a stop, or supposedly had.

Then following, slowly he lifted his lids while cautiously peering into a blur, the light of day. Similar in action would be the comparison of grandma lifting her window shade ever so slowly, not wishing for the sharpness of an overabundance of light to enter at this instance.

Carefully peeking out, and at the same time swinging his legs over the bed's edge talking to himself, he croaked, "I'm Rudy and I will survive - come hell or high water I'll show her - I'll have the high hand in the end." He smiled at himself thinking, *Then me and my Princess, we'll waltz across Texas, we darn sure will.* Then doubt clouded his mind; it was kind of fragile, ya know. The reason for his misgivings is to say, the continual recurring questions that sported doubt his way pestering his thinker, such as: "Or am I just trying to fool myself? Hey, dummy, I'm talking to you, do you hear me?" Rudy would identify with this sketch often yelling at himself more frequently than not! The questions having the same gist only worded a slight difference. The answer, constantly consistent being continually the same -and for that reason - he wonders if he really believed his answers or merely desired them to be just. Or maybe, just maybe, with being alone he was simply trying to convince his heart that there was a larger percentage of possibility than probability.

Well, the decision was made; as a result, he hoped for the best and pulled his Wranglers on one leg at a time. It is important to point out the one leg operation and here is an explanation of why. He had heard stories of drivers sitting on the edge of their beds starting both feet through their respective legs simultaneously. Once they would get each leg started most of the way through the pant legs they would stand up and shortly following they would jump as high as possible kicking both legs while pulling on the waist of the jeans resulting in the success of donning their Wranglers. Rudy tried this one time and vowed never to attempt that trick again. His bed was a bit high therefore touching the floor was an impossibility causing an impromptu jump from the bed with the following explanation. He did jump and at the time of liftoff suddenly decided he would adjust a two step agenda to a one step agenda. Rudy's split decision turned out not to be the wisest of choices to have made. Allow me to explain. When lifting off he undertook the challenge of pulling the jeans up with one motion. This was a feat that should not have been attempted for when he hurdled and pulled, his feet stuck in the pant legs. In reference, reiterating Rudy's balance not being equivalent to that of the conveyor of this feat, therefore that in mind, this action causing him to lunge forward landing flat on his face. The crash landing was not an intentionally managed realization. During the interim, Rudy became wedged between the boundaries of the seats with his arms pinned to their respective sides. After an interim of squirming and consciously keeping his temper under wraps so as not to panic and become claustrophobic, Rudy managed to become free once again. With much effort expended, he struggled to his feet completing his dress and finished the undertaking of readying himself for the day by brushing his teeth and combing his hair. He always had to be presentable, if possible, he thought so anyway. Next, he stepped out of his domain; to most it would be referred to as a truck, but it was all he had to is name, so referring to it as his domain was automatic, a natural pass on.

To continue, he did a walk-around inspection, bumping all eighteen tires finding them sufficiently aired in conjunction with the lights working properly. This was customary and done out of habit for it was a procedure he completed every time he had been stopped for any length of time. As he finished the inspection, Rudy suddenly realized his old Peterbilt was not idling. "What now?" a question posed to himself!

Chapter Two

T HE HAPPENINGS TO FOLLOW WERE the start of an ordeal, a test that would generate laughs from memories whether it would be in the near or distant future. The problem facing Rudy was plain and simple. He had parked on an incline to the east and his truck was facing north. The fuel had run from the right tank to the left tank via the crossover fuel line between the tanks. The problem arose as the fuel for the engine was pumped from the right tank and what was not used was returned to the left tank. It doesn't take a rocket scientist to conclude he had run out of fuel. The incline had caused the fuel to eventually become displaced from the right tank to the left tank consequently causing the engine to die.

"What next?" He thought he remembered seeing a truck stop a mile or so back down the road or it seemed he had and luck hadn't vanished entirely for he remembered the phone number he'd read on a billboard as he sailed past. At that particular time, Rudy carried a cell phone and his luck seemed to be holding; well, for now, because he had a signal.

Bringing to light that phone number, a figure his conscious groped for rummaging through the pits of his mind. Luck was tagging his shirt tail for when entering it into the keypad, with his breath held and trying to imagine his recollection not failing him Rudy's hope was rewarded, the phone started ringing and which gave life to a momentary flash of tranquility. It was only momentary for the ring, ring, ringing went on indefinitely causing Rudy to think it just may never stop. It seemed no one would ever answer. Then finally there was a voice, a female voice, that calmed him, but only fleetingly when it said, "Your party is not answering. Check your number or dial 0 for operator assistance. Thank you for using XYZ for your telephone needs. Thank you, and good-bye." Then promptly Rudy was disconnected. His ears turned bright red, he was sure, for he was prone to that characteristic when his temper got a little bent. Following, he then struggled to stay calm as he possibly could. It more likely than not would have been possible to have seen him chattering to himself saying, "No doubt a Democrat must've designed that feature. Do you suppose I really needed a recorder to inform me that my party was not answering? Don't you suppose I might have noticed? Like duh!"

He dialed it again for there was no other option. After what seemed to be an eternity a voice came on the telephone. "Helllllo." Immediately he responded, "Hello, is this the truck stop?" Then the voice, a female voice said, "Well, baabbeeeey, it sure ain't the Holiday Inn Express! What'cha want?" It was difficult keeping his composure for instinctively he knew he was speaking with someone who was a bit short in the area of gray matter! Rudy collected his wits and replied, "I need your road service to bring me some fuel." In the next breath, Rudy went on informing her of his whereabouts and her reply was music to his ears when she replied, "I would love to bring you some fuel."

These words were a sweet serenade, so not being able to contain himself, he, with much vigor, shouted, "Hallelujah! I'm in luck." Then after screaming his response he went on to speak in a more controlled level voice saying, "Great. How long and how much will it cost for a service call?" Then she replied, "It will cost you $100 for the service call plus the cost of the fuel and labor for priming and starting your rig." Rudy retorted, "Isn't that a little steep?" The woman then declared, "Yeah, I suppose it is but yer gonna have take it or leave it. That's all I can do for you." Then quickly following came, "For now anyway!" Then it came, that snicker and giggle that had an inappropriate evocative tone causing a shiver to run up Rudy's spine. He continued at the same time trying to conceal his discontent declaring, "I suppose I'll have to. I don't have another choice, so how long will it take?" Her response was, "Floyd will be there around 6:00 p.m." Once again, Rudy for a bit got excited and said, "Good, that's only about thirty minutes." The joy that he felt proved to be only momentary when she cackled like a sitting hen that has just laid an egg informing him, "That's not 6:00 p.m. today, honey child, that's 6:00 p.m. tomorrow. You see, Floyd had to use the service truck to take his nephew fishing. Ya see? Floyd hasn't seen his nephew for three years, ya know, so ya see, he just took the service truck. Ya know how it is, I'm sure, and he just left. If you were in his situation, you'd do the same I bet. Wouldn't cha? Well, wouldn't cha? I bet cha would, wouldn't cha!? Huh, not answering, that's fine. I know you would anyway, wouldn't cha?"

Then, Rudy, having a time controlling his temper, came back with, "Good gosh, what's your boss's name?" Then she said, "You don't want to know."

Rudy was about to blow a gasket when he retorted, "Look it here, if I didn't want to know, I wouldn't have asked. Now, what is your boss's name? I'm going to initiate a call informing him of the incompetent help he has robbing him."

"Go ahead make a complaint," she dared, "Just see if it does you any good. It ain't gonna!"

"What is his name and number? Tell me right now!" Rudy exclaimed.

"Where you from? New York or somewhere like that?" she quizzed and went on with, "You could use your manners if you have any and I don't think you do. You are a rude man, yes siree, rude, rude, rude, mighty rude. I ain't ever dealt with someone so rude!"

Rudy could see in a heartbeat that he was going to have to manipulate her into recognizing and believing he really was a nice guy. So, against his will, he decided to apologize then continued by saying, "I am very sorry and hopefully you will allow me the courtesy of expressing my sincere regret. I get consumed with personal problems and forget other people have feelings also. I am sorry!"

That's when I heard her voice saying very unsure like, "Wellll, ookayy. I'll accept it this time, but don't let it happen again. Besides, I guess all bodies make mistakes occasionally. So, if you must know, the boss's name is F. F. Fichen and his phone number is 1-800-279-2229. If ya can't remember the number, the letters spell 1800-cry-baby for people like you. Excuse me like you almost were." She laughed once again.

"What does the F stand for?" Rudy asked.

Then her fanatical laughter! She snorted through her nose and sounded like she was snoring, gasping for air. She continued in such a way that convinced Rudy once again that she may be lacking a few molecules of one complete brain cell as she relayed to him, "The first F is for Fearless, which is a nickname, and the second F is the first letter of his real first name but is used for his middle name and that being Floyd. Fichen is his last name and Fearless Floyd's a-fishing so call him all you want, if you want, but like I told you, it will do you no good to call because Fearless Floyd Fichen is simply not here he's a-fishin'." Then she laughed and laughed and laughed, "Saying, "Did ya get it? Ya know how it sounds the same, his name, did ya get it? Huh, did ya?" She was laughing out of control for she was amused at the similarity of the boss's name and what he was engaged with at that time. Rudy was on the verge of losing his composure, imagine that. The laws of nature or maybe life still seemed to be against him and a bit more than he felt he deserved. Rudy then went on and asked her if she had a couple of buckets he could borrow to carry diesel to his rig.

She came right back with a, "Sure I do, buckaroo, what kinda truck stop do you think you're dealing with anyway, Buster?"

Rudy nearly told her then stopped himself for it didn't seem fair that people were born so mentally inadequate and determined it didn't take all kinds, there simply were all kind. At which time, he decided it wasn't fair to have a battle of wits with an unarmed person. No, it plainly wasn't fair to take advantage of a person so out to lunch as this woman apparently was. So, he reneged on the premise of countering instantly for the reason mentioned previously. Life just isn't fair and suddenly Rudy had a flashback glimpsing a not too distant memory that addressed this same issue and deciding then too that no it wasn't fair, no not at all.

Next, he with much effort replied, "Well, ain't that a wonder … I mean wonderful. I'll hoof it up to your truck stop. It'll be a bit, but I'm on my way. Thanks. Good-bye."

The plan was to carry ten gallons of fuel the distance by hand but was a tad bit disconcerting to say the least. In the interlude reflecting, and once again lurking, anxiety nearly getting control when mulling over the proposition. Rudy supposed he'd better get to doing or he would never get 'er done. Convinced, he readied himself for the trek.

Chapter Three

ONCE THE LACING OF HIS Air Jordans was complete, Rudy locked the doors and set out for the truck stop. He jogged, walked, jogged and intermittently traveled in this fashion until arriving at the destination of mind.

Wheezing for the lack of oxygen, such precious commodity it is, on that account in passing his breathing was more than just a little ragged. He completed the mile trek to the truck stop in a fashionable amount of time but still the time spent a bit more than he would have preferred, but satisfactory, nearly in gist. At which time, Rudy realized just how out of shape he in fact was so he owned up to this piece of evidence that exercise was a necessary adjustment and must be included into his daily routine starting one of these times real soon. It was hard to believe that he'd let himself get so soft. A thought came to Rudy with a stifled chuckle. "Hell, someone had to do it." He smiled at himself accepting this bit of wisdom - an idiom - and its use as commonplace knowing it was more regular than not.

Once gaining his poise, Rudy gazed around and struggled in mind trying to decide what his next option was and where he might look for the dimwit he had spoken with earlier. He didn't even inquire of her name, but he'd bet it was Mabel or something along that line, and suddenly a thought, her name was probably Flo! You know, birds of a feather flock together.

All of a sudden, he decided that breakfast would be a great way to get the day started and headed for a door with a big restaurant sign over the entrance. Standing a step beyond the door when entering, he peered around letting his eyes become accustomed to the interior and at the same time assessing the inside, a natural thing to do when entering an unfamiliar structure. Then the ambiance that addressed him as his vision became familiar with its setting was nearly disturbing in a positive manner. While becoming familiar he took notice of the mood filling the room. A mood that accented all that was good and that caused him to momentarily forget his predicament.

Consistent with Rudy's bewilderment was a woman, a very pretty woman, but then he reneged that exposé instantly when deciding beautiful was a more fitting portrayal. She sported a breathtaking smile, approached and addressed him with a, "Hello, my name is Pricilla. Will you be dining alone or will someone be joining you?" This casual welcome completely different than anything he had ever experienced in the past when embracing a truck stop with his presence and the persona of this exquisite young hostess caused him to pinch himself checking to see if he'd wake up from a dream only to experience another disappointment. She at first seemed to be so, so, so incredibly pleasant as opposed to many who present themselves as doing you a favor. You know, being at your service and operating with an attitude. Deliberately copping a stance that would silently but quite deliberately inform you as to where the exit could be found and not to allow the door to hit your ba-tooty on the way out. Everything important is - in their minds - being about themselves. They would be explained as psychologically inept or out to lunch and for that reason alone being incapable of appreciating the customer and lacking knowledge that without the clientele, they would not have jobs.

People having indiscretions as mentioned in no way would benefit themselves and almost certainly, simply the opposite!

Rudy was taken back through all the years of rodeos and trucking, yet never ever had he been in a truck stop that was graced with such eloquence. She said, "Sir, are you all right?" "Oh yes, yes I'm sorry, excuse me I'm sorry, I was thinking and realizing something. Pardon me for being so rude! I am very sorry. Oh yes, you asked me a question?" "Yes, I was wondering if you are by yourself or if someone is going to be joining you." She repeated herself with eyes dancing and having a tinge of mischief in them. The sun was shining through an easterly window with a compilation of bright rays complementing her beautiful dark brown hair (a brown that was only a shade or two from being described as black) while shimmering from her neck was a string of pearls. "Yes, ma'am, I mean, no, ma'am, I am alone," Rudy said. Then she said, "Walk this way, please." As she turned, she motioned him to follow. Well, him only being human so as he followed her, he couldn't help but notice her body type and made the decision instantly that her Wranglers must be tailored for never had he ever seen the W's on the hip pockets of a pair Wranglers look so incredulously finger licking good. Her remark was to walk this way, please. Heck fire, that old cowboy couldn't walk like that if he tried all of his remaining days, so he simply followed along to her table of choice. He said he believed that was what she intended anyway, just to follow her, and thanks for the small niceties in life for the view was outstanding. It was more than that; it was as Tony the tiger would say, "It's Grrreeaat!"

Rudy had made a request of being seated in a corner for he preferred sitting with his back in that position of a room, most surprises weren't able to sneak up on a guy. They tend to do that every now and again, ya know.

She seated Rudy while informing him his waitress would be there shortly to address his needs. He thanked her when at the same time she was moving away. Smiling and at the time wrinkling her nose ever so slightly, she replied, "You are most welcome. Later!" Then immediately Rudy wondered if there could or maybe would be a later somewhere someday? He watched those W's gracefully be gone while shadows would engulf and prevent the view from his personal scrutiny, while remaining was fantasies delight, man-o-man, what a sight!

In a relatively short period of time his waitress presented herself making Rudy conscious of her name, it being Peggy. With formalities completed, she continued and asked the usual questions regarding what he wanted to drink. Rudy went on to say his scripted remark, "Coffee and water, please." Now she was a case but a nice case, bouncy and smiling ear to ear continually. Freckles on her cheeks and long braids that fell over her shoulders reaching well below her belt line a good six inches or more. Rudy was always amazed how a girl or woman could put up with all the extra effort it took caring for her hair when it was so terribly long.

"Don't get me wrong," Rudy had instructed then went on to say! "Heck fire, I love that women wear their hair long to such a degree. It's a fashion, you know, long hair as such, and it will never ever be outdated. No siree Bob, long hair on women will never be outdated. Too it is my tendency to be partial to this style and more likely than not it is more appealing to me than any other living man."

In a short moment, Peggy had coffee and water to him then inquired as to what he'd like to order for breakfast. "Just kidding," he said, "What you likely do not have."

She didn't hesitate when she replied, "Try me."

So being challenged, he said, "I would like eggs and bacon, but I want the eggs to be fried in bacon grease in a cast iron skillet. I want the skillet to be smoking hot when you drop the eggs in the grease, then salt and pepper 'em and put a lid over 'em. Get a little water and throw under the lid to make the grease really splatter. The grease will splash all over the eggs, causing them to blister and cook the white and I mean all the white in the eggs. Because the skillet is so hot a crust will form around the edge. Once you put the water in the skillet with the grease it will only take about ten seconds to get the desired effect. Do you suppose you can handle that?"

She replied, "I thought you were going to ask me to do something difficult. That is not a problem. No, sir, not at all.

Sir, would you care for anything else?" She caught Rudy a bit off guard for he figured his request to be denied.

Rudy sort of chewed his words when he said, "Oh, yeah! - Yeah, yeah, yeah, sourdough toast would be nice too, please."

Again, Peg came with a reply not hesitating in the least. "Okay, will do. I figured you for a sourdough bread kinda guy. That'll be easy, be back in a short."

Never and He added, never ever had he ever had that type of luck ordering breakfast in his entire life.

After Peggy left Rudy's side, he set to rolling his fingers on the table. First, the little finger or pinky, then his ring finger, to his middle finger, which is probably the most used finger in sign language when wanting to express displeasure with someone and letting them know in no seemed,uncertain terms they are number one. In your book anyway ... not! Last, his pointer or nose picker. First one way, then back the other way. Rudy would do this back and forth for exercise with the intention of it helping the fine motor movement proportional to the coordination of his handicapped arm.

Astounding, for the table was made from a hard wood and each finger made a definite thud when contacting its top. So, enthused in his self-imposed therapy, he nearly jumped out of his skin when she - he implies - snuck up behind him declaring, "Your breakfast is served, sir." She giggled as if she had planned her return just as it happened. With Rudy being so intrigued by the atmosphere of this out-of-the-way truck stop restaurant and too once again enforced the necessity of bringing to light his therapy session. This was a session that dominantly occupied his wherewithal. Therefore, Rudy reiterated he was very startled when she seemed to appear out of the blue. She acted completely innocent of the incident by saying, "Oh, I'm sorry! Did I scare you?" Peggy went on to giggle with a blameless look. Rudy alluded to the fact that he was sure the intent was intentional, and she was attempting to put herself clearly above and beyond suspicion. He then told her not to worry about it, and you know what? Rudy was just pretty darn sure it never crossed her mind again. Why? He didn't know but stated it's just a feeling he happened to have. Right, wrong or?

He then focused on the meal and was quite impressed saying you'd have thought his dad had come back from the beyond to cook those eggs so perfectly. You talk about spuds being cooked right; man, those hash browns were perfect. They had fried them to where they were a little crispy and a brown that was close to being to brown but was in the realm of being cooked perfectly. Someone in that kitchen knew how to cook! There was no doubt about it.

Rudy's place was set with jelly and honey galore. The toast was Texas size.

The bacon was hand cut and the pieces were probably a quarter inch thick, a foot long and six slices. He then eagerly opened and lay his napkin crossways over his lap and placing the other, there were two of them, beside his plate. His next quest was to view the setting, then to decide just where he was going to make a start at satisfying a hunger that had been growing for a time. Taking a sip of his coffee, seemingly it had a richer more satisfying flavor than what he could readily recall.

Rudy spread jelly on one piece of toast that paved the way for putting honey on one of the others. With that bit of preparing his breakfast complete, he sprinkled more salt and pepper on his eggs, including a pretty good dose of Tabasco sauce and too, a bit of ketchup.

He sat stirring his taters into his egg yolks and had just taken a bite of bacon. His left hand held a piece of toast readying it for a bite and that's when it came. A scream that would have raised the dead!

Chapter Four

RUDY REITERATED HIS SEATING REQUEST regarding table choice and its position. His desire of preference was need without question, a location to be in the corner of the room. Once again, he inferred it being necessary to sit with his back to the wall. Inherently a trait developed from past days when watching over his shoulder was the only way to stay healthy. Therefore, the reasoning, then following he vocalized gently but sternly this reminder so there would be no doubt about it. Rudy just couldn't feel comfortable positioned with his back facing the door. He simply wanted to view who ever loomed in his direction when being in a public arena. He vowed that his view must entail being able to see those who would be inclined to threaten his solitude whether in a roundabout way or by design his feet. This action triggered his coffee to spill and his hardly-touched breakfast to go flying and too his table went careening off the elevated portion of the dining area that set above the steps.

All this for the frenzied scream, a begging scream, pleading for assistance. The shrieking went something to the effect of "Help! It's that little waitress. He's a roughing her up, yanking her braids. She needs help! Help her, someone, help her; she needs help. Help her, she needs help." The plea ongoing and insistent, that urgency was the call of the minute, time and again begging for someone to lend a hand but still no one lifted a finger to assist in any way.

With Rudy in stance, he would then amble in the direction of the commotion trying not to draw attention to himself. More out of curiosity than any single thing.

He had just intended to be a spectator like the others but as luck would have it, his interest as innocent as it was backfired. Trying not to draw attention to himself, he took a quick look see one last time and found what he knew would be the case, and that was still no one initiated a helping hand. It was only commonplace to do so when there was a need but a good deed of such lay in concealment. Unjust it may seem, but the case right or wrong had been made so needless to say he was beaconed to the ongoing mess!

Someone hollered, "What the heck's going on?" Instantly came an answering shriek, "It's Peggy! It's that big dude, old man Fichen's nephew, he's got her down and he's a puttin' a hurtin' on her." "Hey," someone yelled, "Help her, he's—!!?"

Next was a consequence of the many years of stern notation by his father and was an education that will not likely ever be forgotten. Rudy's father taught him to respect women and insisted to be so always and he meant always as in every time, no matter what the case was to protect and stand up for them. He said it was his obligation as a male species to protect them when being violated mentally or physically. Therefore, that ingrained without another thought of what the end product may be, his parakeet ba-tooty flew into action. How Rudy could be thinking about the lily-livered cowards as he pushed his way through the crowd was beyond him but that was the case.

There was a dance floor and surrounding the dance floor were tables sitting one after another placed in a well thought out manner for service to the customers and stationed to be beneficial to the patrons.

The dance floor narrowed to a width of single file on each side of the bandstand to allow clientele a small opening to be used to come from and go to the floor as they so desired. The bandstand located directly in the center and raised above the floor made it possible to waltz, rumba or tango under it additionally fulfilling intentions of reaching the other side.

There were stairs on four sides making the top accessible to those with a need to rise to the elevated level. This is where it becomes important to realize Rudy would have to surprise the big galoot putting Peggy in harm's way. When getting within eyeshot, he immediately saw no one was helping her. Understanding why just wasn't there and that being what it was Rudy figures are the reason his instincts kicked in.

He started to the top of the bandstand then surveyed the situation and evaluated the need for crucial and immediate action. One look is when he instantly knew what must be done, for the big galoot's back was to him and Rudy had to move swiftly or something dreadful was probably going to happen. Him not wanting to waste another second so next came a jump that to this day he supposes if pondering the outcome, he could not have justified making, but he didn't and so he did. Leaping with all the energy and strength he could muster and to everybody's surprise, he landed on this big dude's shoulders with the back of his head against the trophy belt buckle he sported. It being one buckle of many he had won in his earlier rodeo days. Rudy clamped his legs around an oversized massive neck in a scissor hold squeezing for everything he was worth.

The overgrown interloper reached up and grabbed Rudy and with this change in strategy little Peggy scampered away with the quickness of Speedy Gonzales. Yes, beep-beep she was out of there. His viselike mitts grabbed Rudy's legs, and according to the story's venue, Rudy ventured to say his eyes bugged out a good inch. Life as he knew it was a pending factor and doubtful to proceed in its accustomed manner unless he were to succeed at getting this big man under enemy control, so he hung on for his dear life. Rudy attempted to run his hands under the giant's chin while continuing the squeeze of the neck with his legs. He gave it his best shot but to no avail for the massive neck was only about as long as a hand was wide, thus with Rudy sitting on his shoulders with legs around his neck there was not enough room to get a grip. The Giant galoot had very large ears and what Rudy did next was grasp hold of them clasping one in each hand like there would be no tomorrow and if he didn't hold on there just may not be. He started spinning trying to shake Rudy by whirling around and around trying to dislodge him from his perch, expecting and hoping the g-forces would assist in displacing Rudy from his roost. Rudy was getting dizzy without a doubt hanging on with every bit of zest for life he could muster. His luck seemed to be on an upswing, too, this sizeable individual was getting dizzy in accordance to his spinning about. All of a sudden, the Goliath of a man started staggering being sporadic in his carriage. He lunged one way and then back the other way and finally stopped in his tracks. At last standing in one spot, his arms dropped to his sides. On the release of Rudy's legs, they immediately felt thankful, that is if an appendage can be grateful for anything, they no doubt were.

Rudy leaped from his shoulders and staggered to a table and sat down. Checking his watch, he was amazed when he noticed immediately that hardly five minutes had displaced from the time of executing his heroism.

Gathering all the air he could muster he tried to yell, "Get a rope! We gotta tie up this big moron." Truth be known, he could hardly speak but someone must have understood him for a yell went up saying get a rope. Pretty soon, all a man could hear was continuing pleas for a rope.

"Here comes another cowboy, and he has a rope," someone yelled.

Rudy started to rise to see what was doing and if he'd be able to help. Then there came a whirring sound and he was jerked abruptly back into his seat. Not knowing what was happening, Rudy nearly panicked but the hair on his neck lay back as it should when he heard that laugh. A laugh, it was an obnoxious laugh and one Rudy couldn't have mistaken so needless to recount for recognition was apparent and immediate. He would have known that hee haw anywhere at any time in the whole world. It was his old buddy, Ben. How things happen to the benefit of a situation was beyond him, but he was one happy camper. The rope that had him hog-tied was that of a team roper and immediately he understood where it came from when hearing that laugh.

Rudy went ahead and squirmed out of his predicament regarding the rope that had immobilized him. It was a situation that needed to be addressed immediately if not sooner. Rudy set gasping for air even though the uncontrolled hunger for the precious commodity of oxygen was lessening. He was so short of air that the energy spent shouting the few orders about getting some rope only made the oxygen shortage more real. Rudy attempted to be short and to the point when informing Ben, "We must get the big galoot outside and horns waggled!"

Rudy hesitated briefly then asked, "Where in blazes did you come from, Ben?"

"Well, it's like this, son. I stopped to grab a bite to eat and had just stepped through the door. As I was closing it there came all this yelling about get a rope, get a rope. 'Hey, cowboy, you got a rope? If ya do, get it, would ya?' Yeah, sure, I do. Who wants to know? Then someone said, 'There's trouble inside!' and they're hollering for a rope, so I got my rope. When I got to the commotion, I saw what, what was, and saw your sorry carcass planted on that chair and couldn't resist doing what I did, end of story."

Before Rudy could get his self-control in a stabilized manner, the big bully started to gain consciousness. With the big man coming to, he felt a chill creeping up his back. He jumped up and yelled, "Get me some twine or rope and dang it put a hurry on. We gotta get this guy tied before he comes to or we'll be in a world of hurt. I ain't ever seen a human moose like him in my life. Hurry up with that rope."

Before more rope was acquired, true to form, Ben hollered, "Come on, Rudy, let's take this gorilla for a ride!" With that being the plan, it left no time for discussion. Ben grabbed one leg and encouraged me to hurry by saying, "Get it in gear, Rudy. Grab his other leg and let's go."

Rudy got a hold of the other strut, then it was one-two-three go. And they did just that. It took a couple of steps to get him moving. *Man,* Rudy was thinking, "I bet if he weighed a pound, he weighed 500 pounds", but once they got 'em moving it seemed to be all downhill from there. They managed to keep their energy going in the appropriate direction while heading for a different exit than the one which they had entered. Across a polished hard-wood floor and out the door they went. Someone helped the duo just a tad and held the door open for as by now they were flying as they went down the steps. The big man's head, bounced down the steps one step at a time bop-bop-bop. If he wasn't prone to headaches before he more likely than not would be now.

Pulling up short of his pickup, Ben retrieved another rope and made short work of securing their newfound challenger.

Leaning against the pickup, they were at odds as what to do with this big whatever he was. They were about to call the law when all of a sudden, a city cop car came flying in then skidded about ten feet before coming to a halt.

In the next breath, Ben said, "Looky there, Rudy. Cops! I never thought I'd ever be glad to see a copper in my life."

However as jubilant as they were, their excitement was short-lived as the police skidded to a stop, their doors flew open, guns drawn and were leveled directly at Rudy and Ben, hollering "Hands up, boys, you're under arrest."

"WHAT? Who? Us?" they chimed in unison!

Chapter Five

"UNDER ARREST? EXCUSE US, OFFICERS, but you're arresting the wrong guys," Rudy hurriedly said. They wasted no time in telling him, "Yeah, I'm sure. I know you troublemakers and you are all the same. Ya try and blame your wrongs on seemed,anyone else but yourself." Ben started to speak, but they immediately told him to shut up. That was the wrong thing to do for no one told Ben to shut up without some sort of repercussions, not even the law.

Ben had that look on his face. A look Rudy had only seen a couple times in his life as he sidled over to the cops wagging his finger first at one then the other and very plainly and simply let them know that he didn't start any trouble, but he could finish it and there may be a continuation of the finish if they didn't get their attitudes adjusted. His swagger included an air of don't push your luck, Bud Row, and it was just a part of him. Rudy had witnessed this a time or two before and rather they knew it or not they had better give their attitude a monumental overhaul. Ben was a man of means, which included money and having old cronies who were connected in certain places that most normal people wouldn't ever have the pleasure of knowing these people existed. That being a fact, he had no fear of consequences.

One cop reached out to grab Ben and from a reflex action he batted the cops had away and said, "That's once. You try that again and I'll have your dollar and twenty-five cent job, little man. Dig the wax out of your ears and listen to what I've got to say." Some way or another they got the drift of what Ben was driving at and became all ears. After explaining what had happened, the coppers became a bit dignified and evolved to become officers of the law instead of Barney Fife or Rosco P. Coltrane.

Once an understanding had been reached, they requested Rudy and Ben's service with regards to getting this big boy, rather man, in the police car. An undertaking that shouldn't have been difficult but big man was so massive a blind man could have seen he wasn't about to fit through the cruiser's door. Looking around trying to weigh their options the cops were shaking their heads with that helpless look like a little kid who had just messed his pants.

This oversized character had been lying as if he would never come to then suddenly, he started to do just that. He mumbled something about having to get up and needed to get going before his uncle found out about him being a bad boy. After listening to him babble his concerns of getting in trouble, it only took Rudy a couple of seconds to put two and two together and decide the big feller was a few marbles shy of having a full bag. He went into one of his fear featured all over the place ramblings, asking as near as Rudy could tell, "Am I goin' to jail? Don't let 'em put me in jail, would'ja, mister, would'ja please? Don't let 'em put me in jail. My uncle will beat me! Please don't let them put me in jail." As he became more coherent his gibberish of this and that sent a feeling of helplessness over Rudy and for that reason he felt sorry for this big kid. Actually, he was not awfully old and Rudy had an unexplainable feeling that he actually wasn't as dumb as first thought.

Talking about lethally dangerous, this person with a child's mind and having a Frankenstein size and strength was lethal weapon 13. The next catch-22 was what they were going to do with him.

Rudy, being soft hearted, gullible or possibly a tad bit soft between the ears, got him to settle down. Out of nowhere, he said, "Hey, let's throw the big lug in the back of your pickup, Ben." He replied, "Sure, why not?" At that, Ben took charge of the situation as if the policemen were not even present.

Ben all of a sudden realized he didn't even know this big kid's name, so he asked, "Hey, bud, guess you ought to tell me your name."

He right away said, "My name is Ernie. My luck but my mother liked Ernie and Burt, what can I say?"

"Ernie it is, and may I call you Ernie?" Ben asked the young giant.

"Darn sure, heck fire, sir, you can call me anything, anything at all," was his reply.

Ben next asked Ernie, "Do they need your hands cuffed or do the cops need their guns drawn? You gonna be good if we untie you?"

Ernie replied, "Heck no, they don't. I'm going with them. I ain't gonna cause them any grief. I'll go of my own free will. I ain't as dumb as some folks think. No, sir, not near as dumb!"

The next thing was to free Ernie. Ben started to untie the young Goliath and out of nowhere those two local cops came a-running. They had an extreme dose of excitement working overtime when clamoring, "What the devil do ya think you're doing there, cowboy?"

Ben looked at them like they were from outer space while asking, "What's it look like, Einstein?"

"Looks like your untying him," Barney said, being rather sure of his accusation.

Then followed with a, "You'd better not do that. I mean, don't you do that."

"There's that attitude once again," Ben observed, trying to learn to tolerate it. "Didn't we have an understanding about throwing orders around? Just in case we didn't we'll have one now. Understand?"

Barney tried to stand there and speak but was tongue-tied, for his better judgment was making an attempt at taking over the situation. "Welllll, don't untie him. He's too big, too strong, he'll cause trouble! He'll get away!"

"Sorry but he promised not to do anything dumb and I'm going to take his word that he won't." This bantering back and forth was processing while Ben finished unraveling the giant's arms and legs.

Once Ernie had gotten his feet under him, he stood straight and tall as he was able then replied, "I ain't gonna cause any more trouble. I promise!"

"Well, gentlemen, you heard the gentle giant speak. He has no plans to cause any trouble, so you can holster your weapons so there's not an accident." Surprisingly enough, they did as Ben requested and slowly but surely, Rudy and Ben followed them to the cells to lock up the big, mean kid who turned out to be in fact a very gentle person who had been bullied and misused all of his life never having anyone to love or be loved by.

The future harbored the start of a new life for a very capable individual by the name of Ernie Fichen. In the meantime, the so-called law wanted to lock him up overnight and Rudy, along with Ben, convinced Ernie it was going to be okay. Then he said, "Cool. I won't have to get a motel room!" Then he flashed a corresponding smile, which would be more correctly described as a big boyish-type grin, with eyes a-dancing.

Chapter Six

VENTURING BACK TO THE RESTAURANT was the duo's next endeavor. Having the intention of checking on and seeing how too Peggy had fared after the fiasco of the earlier debacle. Also, to take notice how everyone was handling the recent calamity. Humiliation, would best describe, that what was over actually before it had gotten started, when regarding Peggy's state of being.

As they stepped inside, Pricilla met them another time with the same managed manner as she had earlier. Another happening that made it a two count and Rudy was nearly transfixed by that elegant smile she once more sported their direction. Man-oh man, why aren't there more women made like this one? Rudy wondered. His admiration must have shown for Ben said in his obnoxious way, "Be careful. Rudy, don't step on your tongue." Then he let go of one of his belly laughs as they followed her to their table and all the time Rudy was glaring at this uncouth being he called a friend.

She seated Rudy; Okay, he supposed it would be more correct to espouse that she seated them not just Rudy once again and by their request in a corner to keep surprises looming elsewhere.

She made use of her usual scripted delivery having to do with their server and her being at their beck and call shortly.

By now it was late in the afternoon, nearly meal time they noticed when glancing at their watches and decided to treat themselves with an early supper. Rudy was well aware the yuppie-duppie crowd would refer to the meal as dinner. *Excuse me for being so adamant about this meal but I believe the proper names for meals are breakfast, dinner and last but not least supper. This is in direct contrast with breakfast, lunch and calling the last meal of the day dinner. Now that I have cleared up that little misconception I must add what we expected was met wholeheartedly,* Rudy thought. Chuck roast was the main entrée that made the saliva run. Included topping it off was a dessert of apple pie with homemade vanilla ice cream that was so delicious that Miss Piggy would have squealed with delight.

Once supper was consumed, Rudy and Ben sat chewing the fat for they hadn't swapped lies for quite some time. They inquired about Peggy and to their liking she was doing well but had been sent home for the remainder of the day which was nearly all day. They were told she intended to return the following morning

They were let down, more than just a little, or Rudy was anyway, because he had hoped to see that vibrant, bouncy freckle face ball of energy one last time. Rudy took notice of who was in earshot of their conversation, then he spoke kind of quietly out the corner of his mouth. "Ya know, Ben, there seems to be something out of sorts here. It has the appearance of something a little more than being a slight bit fishy. I just can't put my finger on it, but too putting it out of mind is not an option either."

Ben replied, "I was thinking the same thing, Rudy. Ya know we ought to hang around here a day or two. Whattaya think 'bout that? We might have to get into a wild beer drinking contest or girl chasing quest or maybe both. Whattaya think about them apples?" He hee-hawed like a mule.

"Hell, why not?" Rudy managed to spit out between trying not to burn his tongue from his coffee and laughing at Ben.

"Let me tell you about Ben, when he got in one of his moods, you never saw a man who had a bigger smile and he smiled with every tooth in his head. His eyes were just a-jumping and a-shining. The only thing that would register in my mind was a question of what our meeting may bring and I was wondering if I should start worrying now or later. With assorted effort I was able to put my thoughts to rest."

Suddenly Ben looked at Rudy and asked, "How the heck did you get here?"

Rudy stammered and stuttered trying to make up a reason to explain what had happened. His attempt of an explanation or excuse would probably be more accurate was less than feeble. Ben smiled looking at Rudy and said, "Rudy, yer a feedin' me a bunch of malarkey. Just give it to me straight, would ya?"

So, Rudy told him what had happened. He expected Ben to give him his usual bunch of grief but to Rudy's astonishment he was stunned by Ben's reaction, which was that of feeling sorry for Rudy for when he completed Ben simply said, "Man, it never lets up for you, does it?"

Ben's remark sort of threw Rudy so the only thing he could think to say was, "I guess not but one thing is for sure it'll get better now. There's only one way to go now and that's the right way. Getting rid of that 180-pound dead weight is a blessing and never again will I ever have an anchor of such pure muck that's so intent on dragging me down to their level." Then as an afterthought, he continued with, "And you can take that to the bank. I guarantee it!"

Ben acknowledged his approval but smiled a crooked grin when adding, "She wasn't so bad, was she?" He laughed then went on with, "I heard she was well used but not abused!" Then once again laughed unceremoniously and Rudy squirmed. Then Rudy replied with, "Well, the well-used darn sure is right but not by me. Anyway, no mistake about it if excessive use is abuse then on second thought, she's been severely abused at that." Then they laughed and so hearty was their laughter that sides ached momentarily which for that reason is why their breath was a tad bit in short supply.

Next Ben asked, "Hey, Rudy, you thinkin' about your truck?? You probably gonna need some help getting' 'er started, ain't ya?"

Rudy came back with, "You must be a rocket scientist, and just how'd you figure that out?" He laughed and went on to say, "My plans are your plans, Ben. Ya suppose you might give me a hand? You know, find it in yer schedule to haul some fuel to it?"

"I suppose but it's gonna cost ya dearly," Ben said.

"Tell me something I don't already know, girly man." Rudy prodded him for Rudy knew something about him that not another soul knew. "I guess I'm a-gonna hafta start a nasty rumor around about you wearing women's underwear!"

Ben bristled almost immediately saying, "You wouldn't do that?"

"Try me," Rudy challenged in good fun.

"You sorry little puke! You know I didn't have a choice but to put them on."

"Sure, sure, sure I do, but things have started to get a bit foggy and beings how I'm the only one who knew or knows," Rudy replied.

"Okay, okay, you win," Ben conceded.

All of this was done in fun to identify silently that they were old friends and would continue to be so for many days to come.

"You got a five-gallon bucket, Ben?" Rudy asked.

"No, I don't. Why? What do ya need a five-gallon can for?" Ben inquired kind of innocent-like.

Rudy walked over and laid his hand on Ben's forehead and asked, "Do you have a case of CRA [Can't remember anything]?"

Rudy put on a pretense of being impatient and answered, "I just told you I ran out of fuel. Now what do you suppose I'd want a bucket for? Like duh! Supper is over, you can return any time."

Ben flashed a one fingered sign telling Rudy he was number one while shaking his head acting like he was full of sympathy for me. "To heck with a bucket, my boy! I've got a tank of diesel in the back of my pickup. Put that in there so I could carry more fuel from home when fuel started gettin' so darn expensive. You know, a penny here, a penny there, every little bit saved helps." "You got that right," Rudy agreed.

"If you're gonna help me, why don't we head to my truck and see if we can have any luck getting it started," Rudy suggested.

Ben came back with, "It ain't gonna be luck, Rudy, you oughta know by this time that it's good old-fashioned knows how." As usual, Ben let his arrogance gently flow.

"Know how, luck, whatever it is, I don't care at this point. I'd just like to getter running."

"Let's hop in my pickup and get on out there and see what it's gonna take to get it fired up," Ben recommended.

"Okay," Rudy said. "Let's do it."

They got in Ben's pickup and headed in the direction of Rudy's truck. Ben wondered out loud, "It's got me mixed up trying to figure out the deal with Ernie. You know, him being related to Old Man Fichen. It just doesn't add up why all the trouble. You know, there has to be more to it than meets the eye."

"You know, Ben, I've been thinking the same as you. I think we should stick around a day or two like we talked about earlier and investigate this bunch of crazies. Something just ain't right here. I think it be up to us to find out what that something is."

"Well, imagine that! We agree on one thing anyway!" Ben said.

"Here we are. You got a new truck since the last time we crossed paths," Ben stated.

"Well, Ben, I didn't know you had a running tally on my trucks, but yes, trading trucks a while back was a choice made for me not because I wanted to but because I didn't have an alternative. My motor dropped, cost me a small fortune to get towed 200 miles back to town. I had a time-sensitive load on it that could not be late so consequently I traded trucks in a hurry. You know Murphy's and Rudy's law. If something can go wrong, it will, and it did, but my new truck is pretty darn nice. It's nice not having a big truck anymore; I've got a large car now," Rudy explained.

Ben asked with a perplexing look across his rugged, questioning face, "I hate to ask, but what's the difference between a big truck and a large car?"

Then, putting Ben in a position of having Rudy explain something as simple as that, Rudy retorted, "You don't know the difference?"

Ben said, "Now do you suppose I woulda asked you if I did?"

"No, I suppose it hurts you to have to ask, doesn't it?" Rudy didn't leave him time to answer and went on to clarify the difference by saying, "Just so you won't look stupid if someone asks you someday. It's like this. A big truck goes as fast as it can and the difference is a large car like mine, well, it goes as fast as it wants to!" Rudy grinned at him.

Ben just shook his head and replied, "I should have known that your answer was going to be something on that order."

"It's a fact," Rudy assured him.

"Yeah, I'm sure probably only in your dreams," Ben contested.

"More than my dreams. It has 550 horses under the hood, 18 speeds with an overdrive transmission and a rear gear ratio of 336.

This truck gives a new meaning to land air," Rudy informed Ben in no uncertain terms. "This baby will fly."

"We'd better get to and see if we can get 'er runnin' or what it's gonna take to make that happen," Ben said. "Or it may deserve a new title like road kill because it is dead and will not wake up."

"Fine by me." Rudy added, "Let's get 'er done." He pretended not to hear the critique of his truck as Rudy preferred Ben to shut up as he did. But not for long.

Chapter Seven

Meanwhile, Barney and Rosco were hashing over the happenings of what had just taken place. A funny twist of fate is their real names were just that, Barney, who deemed himself the leader of the two, and nonetheless, Rosco, who was probably less than none!

Barney was drumming his fingers on the desk and Rosco sat watching quietly. Puzzled at how Barney could do that with his fingers and never miss a beat. About then Barney jumped to his feet blurting out, "Rosco, let's give Ernie a going over."

"You can," Rosco said "I ain't a-gonna get near that human destruction zone."

"Oh, come on," Barney encouraged. "Let's see if we can get under his skin. It'd be funny if he'd wet his pants again. Come on, let's give it a try."

"I don't know, Barney. you know how old fatso Fichen gets when we treat that moron in there like that." Rosco was attempting to roll his fingers like his superior and trying to do so with every bit of try he could muster. A frown appeared on his vacant face that would have made Bimbo the clown laugh.

Ben and Rudy had been working on that stupid truck nonstop hoping to get it running but luck just wasn't on their side. "Man, them Caterpillar engines suck. It's tough, ain't it, bleeding the air from the fuel lines trying to get fuel to the injectors once they are pumped dry?"

I must have sounded like a whiner for Ben came back with, "Yeah, I suppose so but you know what? If someone wouldn't a run it out fuel we wouldn't be having this little conversation, now would we? Pardon me for being so rude, but would you like a little cheese with your 'whine'?" With that snide little quip, Ben once again smiled big, showing off his grinners. His remark shut up Rudy, and the worst thing about it was that he was right so Rudy couldn't say one thing in his defense. To top it off, Rudy had to own up to the fact the engine wasn't stupid, RUDY was. So, another lesson learned.

Rudy was not sure where the time went while working on his truck, but one thing for sure, it went; it just didn't hang around. It got cloudy with the wind picking up more than just a little. With this fact at hand, the guys put the hurry on, for not only was it getting a little breezy, Mother Nature also decided to dim the lights. Yes siree, nightfall was just below the horizon. It was intruding with obnoxious speed and the persistency of Michael Jordan, the Chicago Bulls basketball great. They had to finish in a flash or come back later, which was not the choice of the moment but common sense prevailed and they decided that another day it would have to be.

With that decision made Rudy and Ben picked up and stowed their tools. They jumped in the pickup and made the brief journey back to the truck stop. They debated what their next move should be and couldn't put a finger on what our their stance would exist of. When arriving at town, the guys thought it may be prudent to venture in the direction of the jailhouse to pay Ernie a visit with the intention of assuring him that they would definitely be back in the A.M. to pick him up.

When motoring past the truck stop it seemed quiet and serene when comparing it with the mess it had housed earlier. Its appearance was that of having settled down from the excitement of prior events. It was only a fallacy Rudy and Ben thought it had straightened out. For when they arrived at the jailhouse, they entered and lo and behold, Rosco and Barney were giving the what for to Ernie. They had him on the verge of crying. "Hey, what's going on here?" Ben blurted out.

You would have thought someone had jabbed those two cops in the butt with a needle or something for they jumped up as straight as steel rods. "Oh, nothing. We're just doing a little interrogating," Barney offered.

"Yeah, nothing, nothing at all." Rosco chimed in all the while looking like he had gotten caught with his hand in his pocket playing pocket pool!

Ben came back with, "It doesn't look like nothing to me. What the heck do ya think you're doin', riding' him like that? Do ya suppose you'd like a small portion of that? I could offer up a tad of that dish then we could find out what type of appetite you boys have. Ya know, see if you like the flavor or find out if yer all blow and no go. Just so you know, I'm a master chef of serving that sort of dish. I'm sorry, I just can't help wanting to see what kind of big brave coppers ya guys are. Why don't ya try that stuff on me? You know, feed me a little of that dish."

That's when Barney's ego got the best of him. Hooking his thumbs under his suspenders he started working his way over to Ben, waddling as if his pants were starched rocking from one leg to the other with big steps acting like he was somebody important. He was bloated up attempting to stick his chest out for effect but was hard-pressed to pass along his animated image as being anything more than a full-fledged loser. It had no or little effect other than the fact it was very amusing to witness a grown man acting so out of place. In the meantime, Barney had maneuvered in front of Ben posing his pretense of bravery and trying to stand as tall as his scrawny features would allow. It was futile, the attempt, for he wouldn't have scared a first grader at a Halloween party. He was doing his best when trying to be brave thus infusing a sense of dominance, but Rudy was obligated, or so he thought, to point out he would be yearning for many months for he failed miserably and at his assumed role of importance. As Barney got closer to Ben, his better sense of judgment took charge. Attempting to look Ben in the eye but failed wretchedly. He just couldn't muster the courage to do so and would use his inferior height at a later date as an excuse of why if he was ever questioned about it. Good old Barney took a deep breath then stepped sort of gingerly a little closer and went on to say while looking at Ben's Adam's apple, "See here, bubba, we're the law and, and, we, we can do anything we want so put that in your pipe and smoke it. You go on and get out of here now or I'll be locking you up too."

"Wrong once again!" Ben hotly spun his answer towards Barney. "You couldn't lock old Mother Hubbard up if she didn't choose to be, and let me see, she's been dead forever, so, my friend, don't bite off more than you can chew. Do you like, get the picture, little man?"

Barney, completely at a loss for words, stood and stared at Ben. He had never had a quote unquote civilian show him that type of respect, which was none.

Ben stepped toward Barney saying, "I asked you a question and unless my ears are full of wax or something, I didn't hear your answer. I'll ask one more time, do you get the picture?"

Poor Barney, if you can have sympathy for someone having such a vastly low IQ, simply wilted back as though there was an invisible power pushing him and saying at the same time, "Well,

I'm sorry. We didn't mean nothin'. I was just trying to learn the big kid that it ain't nice to fool with the law. You know, do what he was a-doin' to that little gal, pickin' on her like that and all."

"You chicken sh-" Ben almost slipped but caught himself and said, "C'mon, Rudy, let's split. They've got their warning. Hey, Ernie, stay cool. We'll be back in the morning to get ya out, do ya hear me?"

There then came an answer closely being inaudible or so it seemed. The problem was that Ernie was laughing so hard he hardly had the breath to put forth a reply. He wholeheartedly enjoyed hearing Officer Barney being manhandled verbally as had just happened. He finally was able to deal with the control issue so once getting his breath, answered with a choking, "Ok!" Then all you could hear was an uncontainable laughter like none other than anyone could remember hearing.

The two when stepping into the street said they'd be back in the morning and reinforced their promise when saying, "You can take that promise to Fort Knox, buddy boy, and I don't make idle promises and that is a guarantee!"

Chapter Eight

THEY LOADED INTO BEN'S PICKUP and commenced towards the idea of once again gracing the truck stop with their business. Neither speaking to the other by this time, for they were completely entwined in thought concerning the ordeal with which were faced. As if rehearsed, Rudy and Ben at the same moment looked at each other and in unison spoke, "What next?" Rudy was quick to say, "Well, you seem to be the one with the cornered market concerning brain power, big boy, what you asking me for!" With that pointed out, Ben just wagged his head back and forth started laughing and called Rudy a little son of a something or another and very definitely alluded to the fact Rudy hadn't changed, not even a little bit. Rudy looked at him with his ever so innocent face and was quick to question what he was getting at by saying, "Whatever in the world are you talking about, Ben? Surely you've gotten me confused with one of your other pals. Goodness gracious, I ain't ever been like that whatever like that is." Ben just looked at Rudy and once again started wagging his head back and forth with that big old grin planted on his face relative to a porcupine eating cactus and went on to say, "That's okay, Rudy. You have it your way for now anyway for all good things go home to roost and that is when you'll get yours." Rudy put the thought of that promise out of his mind, for he knew if Ben said it, he meant it, therefore it wasn't the question of if it would be, but when it was going to happen. Ben would be there to deliver the wares, good or bad, you could count on him for he would be there.

Skidding to a stop near the truck stop, Ben rubbed his belly and expressed, "Man, I'm about to starve to death."

"Yeah, you poor little guy. I can hardly see ya when you turn sideways to me." Rudy went on to say, "Heck fire, I bet you're down to a petite 38-inch waist, ain't ya?" He just couldn't help needling Ben for that was the way Rudy was; right or wrong, that was Rudy.

They entered the truck stop and what they had figured proved to be so. That being Pricilla, the provocative hostess, was not on duty. Their surprise was minimal, for heck fire, a person can only work so many hours out of a day.

Standing there probably looking like two bumps on a log for, there was a message board with words written very boldly. Wait to be seated. No please, no thank you, just the words wait to be seated. The word wait was underlined twice to enforce the urgency of this directive. So, they waited, waited and waited some more then finally a short dumpy wee bit of a man greeted them. He was unkempt and his manners were that of a rattlesnake. His personality was not attuned to his predecessor. That in subject Rudy and Ben were some-what disenchanted but came to a conscious decision that help was probably hard to find. Arriving at this decision because the township was a very small, besides, everybody needs a job, so be it, and he had his. The little man said, "Follow me if you want to be seated or just stand like that old what's his name, that old wooden Indian. It makes no difference to me." He grunted.

"Looks like we'll be following you, sir," Rudy was quick to reply. He gave Rudy a sideways look when Rudy called him sir. He had a stunned gaze crossing his pitifully homely face. Near as Rudy could tell or surmise, the look was that of astonishment for apparently no one gave him respect, let alone called him sir. He was caught off guard more than just a little. When Rudy and Ben got to the table, he threw the menus on its top and remarked over his shoulder as he strayed away, "Your waitress will be with you sooner or later but probably more late than soon, like it or leave, it makes no difference, sir." As he stepped away, Rudy caught a faint glimpse of a smile that was trying to flicker as he said sir. Whether he actually carried himself with a bit of dignity in a newly acquired swagger or was simply a state of mind, the mind being Rudy's, it appeared as he did. For now, Rudy had an unexplainable feeling of attainment thinking of this mindless less than adequate human being.

Ben looked like he'd been slapped for he just could fathom how someone could be so incredibly rude. Him not believing what had just happened, he went on to remark, "That little sawed-off piece of democrat dung needs an attitude adjustment. What do ya suppose gives a person such an irresistible personality?" Ben's position of disgust was justified when making an excuse for the little man by merely stating, "Heck, he probably ain't had any for a month or two. I'd guess that's probably why." He countered himself by saying, "A month or two would be in his dreams! I'd say it would probably be more like in this lifetime." They watched him trail away shaking their heads in sympathy, and then he was out of sight.

Patience never was one of Rudy or Ben's virtues so it was senseless to say and for that reason would go unsaid they were annoyed. They sat and waited with aggravation growing as time slowly dissolved.

Ben, out of the blue, spoke up, "Hey, Rudy, whaddaya think really makes a man so irritable as that idiot?"

"Well, my friend, I believe I can answer that question but don't think I probably should."

"Huh, why not?" Ben blurted out.

Rudy hesitated then went on to inform him, "It's an answer I don't suppose you'd agree with."

"Whaddaya mean by that?" Ben challenged.

"You may think I'm losing it, Ben, but I've got a soft spot when encountering someone like him. I'd bet a dollar to a hole in a donut that everyone he comes across gives him more grief than a normal man can imagine. He probably gives himself a hard time. I know basically you're a fair man, Ben, and you do, know what I mean. I know you've given your share of misery to people in his position. I'm not talking a job position, I'm speaking of people who sort of look like that. He simply needs to have someone pound him on the back and tell him good job occasionally. If that were done, I'd bet his attitude would pick up to a positive which would affect the way he felt about himself and sooner than later it would show in his general appearance by how well he kept himself groomed."

"Okay, okay, that's enough of that psychologist malarkey person, Rudy! I had forgotten you were a self-taught shrink who is holier than thou. Remind me to never question your judgment regarding such again," Ben pleaded.

"So be it, but what I just said is a fact and that's what it is, a plain and simple fact! Think about it, Ben, and even you should be able to see what I'm alluding to, to be correct and final!"

"Okay, okay, you're right, Rudy. I know you're right, Rudy, but when aren't cha right, Rudy?" Ben posed repeating Rudy's name again and again for effect. Then, Rudy not wanting to let his approval of wither and be gone couldn't help himself, so capitalizing on the moment. he readily agreed with Ben and said, "Yeah, I guess you got one thing right anyway and it really pleases me that you can own up to that fact. It's hard to be perfect but I suppose someone's gotta be, so it might as well be me." Rudy threw a cross-eyed glance in Ben's direction and if looks could kill, Rudy would be dead. Oh well, they can't, so mark one up for Rudy 'cause he's still very much alive!

"Hey, Rudy!" Ben countered while acting as if they hadn't been in bantering back and forth. "We have to give thought to our friend Ernie and just what we intend to carry out or how we are going to make easier his predicament in the morning."

"Ya know, that little bit of a situation's been raising my hackles a might too. Something just ain't kosher as to what's a-goin' on here. I'm convinced we've got to get to the bottom of it or that poor kid is going to be living a life of pure hell from now til he is only a thought in some other's mind!" Rudy implied.

"Well, we're on the same page or so it seems, so let's put our heads together and come up with a plan," Ben snarled.

Chapter Nine

ERNIE RECLINED ON HIS BED just waiting for Rudy and Ben, his mind a-racing trying to get a handle on what had taken place at the watering trough, his pet name for the bar where trouble had erupted. He was trying but not being to answer his questioning mind. Deciding that taking his punishment like a man would be the only consolation for this pickle he'd gotten himself into. This jail cell was rather confining. He didn't even know what he had done and or rather was accused of doing. He remembered someone saying something about Peggy and him hurting her. Could that be possible, him hurting the one gal he was in love with? He didn't think so and knew one thing for sure. He would never again take another drink that was alcohol spiked. The puzzling part of the unpleasant incident was he couldn't recall taking a drink this time. What was the inexplicable root for his drunken disorderliness or who was behind it? The last time Uncle Floyd was out of town and episode of likeness had taken place, he wondered how in the world such things happened. Ernie lay trying to bring to thought, who or what may have been the mastermind of this inebriated and rowdy conundrum.

Then remembering Ashton Crawford and considering the possibility of maybe, just maybe, him being the culprit. Good old Ashton maybe was responsible for his punch getting laced with a tad bit of

190 proof. Ernie came to the presumption that it had to be something with a kick like that, so with regards to his decision vowed to confront Ashton the first chance of opportunity. He said to himself, "Good old pretty boy Ashton, I'll teach him a thing or two."

Then he being wary of Ben and Rudy, he just couldn't satisfy the misgivings that warned him of the two. But why would they promise to be back the following morning? Why would they promise to return if they intended to do differently? Ernie guessed time would tell and undoubtedly hoped with all his might that their promise of return was genuine and for that reason would return as pledged. He would say a prayer relative to the prediction and hoped it would be enough to right the ill-treatment that was being unleashed his direction. With that thought in mind, Ernie decided to retire with the hope that the night would pass with swift satisfaction! "Man, this bunk sucks." He muttered to himself as he lay trying to find a comfortable position and not having luck this weary evening. Laying, tossing from side to side, hoping for a shot at visiting slumber land but seemingly to no avail. What seemed to be an eternity coming was that of long-awaited voices raised to an excessive volume. There could be no mistake! It was Ben's voice, but Ernic wasn't sure if Rudy was there or not. From the tone of the voice, Ernie decided he'd better be dressed immediately if not sooner. He could hear mostly one voice carrying on hardly slowing for a breath of air. It was saying with a belligerent tone, "Bud-row, I told you I'd be back so iffin' you know what's healthy, I'd get your keys and retrieve your prisoner, like right now, you hear me? Get to it." Ben impressed upon Rosco then shouted at him, "I mean now not tomorrow." Ben leaned over his desk and questioned the befuddled Roscoe in a controlled low, stern and mocking tone, "Do you understand me Roscoe, huh, do ya?" Then he flashed a grin, a malicious intimidating grin with his face only inches away from Rosco's and would more likely than not make a self-assured person doubt himself. Needless to say, because of Ben's daunting way, Rosco was rapidly losing his composure with eyes darting hither and yon wishing for Barney's return.

Ben suddenly slammed down his fist hard in the middle of the desk Rosco was sitting behind. Rosco's eyes opened as wide silver dollars as Ben growled, "NOW!"

Quite startled, Rosco jumped nearly a foot off his chair while stuttering, "Yesses, Sisisirrrr." And still his eyes rushing back and forth hoping for Barney's return. It was a wish that Ben could have told him was not going to happen, for Barney had his hands full with Rudy.

With two thoughts in mind, Ben and Rudy had chosen different directions to explore. They could see no reason to put all their eggs or if you rather chance of choices in one basket or one direction.

The hullabaloo Ben was creating in the jailhouse gave Rudy time to inspect for a proper get away if it came to that. Their flight of departure may need to be complemented with an ingenious effort to handicap those who chose to follow them.

While scouting the outer buildings, Rudy found an old cable and too guessed it to be was approximately 3/8 inches in diameter and maybe 50 feet long, which would suffice perfectly with an idea that arose out of nowhere and wormed its way into his mind.

Rudy was not a roper, like Ben, but had plenty of practice coiling a throw rope so he picked up the cable and immediately coiled it up as such. After this action was complete, he discovered the weight was much more than he had suspected, so he had to put a little umph into carrying it to where the cop car was parked. Rudy, at this time, was walking on the high side of nervousness 'cause he didn't need to be caught doing what was in the back of his head.

Taking a big breath trying to steady his nerves, he walked to the city cop car and threw the cable under the back end. Rudy, at that time, in one motion hit the ground and rolled beneath the car. Thank god for 15-inch wheels, he at a later date expressed.

With speed what seemed like a snail's pace, Rudy tied each end of the cable to separate spots on the front axle close to each front wheel. He then threw the other around the end hitch of an old Caterpillar that was just inches away from the back of the car. The relic Caterpillar was obsolete and parked there to represent the working man, that of which this whole town was made up. Its weight was several tons and would make a perfect anchor to stop the constable's car when leaving in chase of Rudy and Ben or any other person who it was deemed necessary to pursue.

The procedure of booby trapping the black and white only took a few minutes although seemingly it was much longer than that. Rudy had just gotten out from under the car and making himself presentable when he spied Barney strolling along the street just a-whistling as if he didn't have a care in the world. Guilt was running rather heavy across Rudy's mind, so he decided to go on the attack once Barney got within earshot.

"Hey, Barney, whatcha so happy about this morning? Did you win the lottery or something?" Rudy pointedly asked. "I know! I bet you gave your Mama an eviction notice or something, didn't ya?"

Barney looked around sort of nervous like Rudy expected to see if Ben was anywhere to be seen. When he was sure they were the only ones in the vicinity, Barney sucked in all the air he was able to hold and waltzed up to Rudy sticking his chest out as far as Mother Nature would allow. He bellowed, "Boy, I just don't know what I'm going to do with you and that smart mouth of yours. Lucky for you I've gotten my good nature on this morning or I'd be locking you up with that big, fat, good-for-nothing Ernie." Barney further spewed, "And if you aren't careful, I may have to anyway. You know, for good measure. Yep, plainly for good measure. Do you want that to happen? Boy!"

At that exact instant Rudy caught a glimpse of Ben and Ernie stepping from the jailhouse into threshold area that was covered by an awning.

Chapter Ten

IN THE INSTANCE OF PREPARING the groundwork that would put a halt to the cops' pursuit, Ben rattled Rosco so that he didn't know if he was coming, going, or had just gotten there or was preparing to leave. Persuading Rosco to give him the lockup keys, he then opened the jail cell door. This jail was like the one in The Andy Griffith show. Ernie was quite ready to be released and came out of that cell faster than the bullet from a 7-millimeter Magnum deer rifle.

Once free from what he described as his captors' imprisonment, Ernie sauntered over to Rosco and looked down his nose and witnessed a terrified, pathetic, inadequate law man and went on to say, "Come on, little man, you and I have an issue to be discussed." Rudy virtually felt a bit of remorse for the poor misdirected little law man. He wasn't sure what Ernie was going to do with him and was surprised when Ernie simply ushered him into the cell he had just vacated then abruptly turned and all in one motion stepped out and shut the door while hanging the cell keys on a peg that projected from within the wall that separated the two cells. The keys, like the keys Matt Dillon used in GunSmoke, a long-running TV show, and too being just out of reach from Rosco's grasp.

Ben stood and watched Ernie proceed about his business and was nearly speechless with the quiet and grace that had engulfed the big kid.

Simultaneously they looked at each other and spoke to one another in the same breaths with Ben saying, "We'd better get to gettin'." And Ernie asking, "What's next, Boss?"

Boss! Heck fire, no one had called Ben boss for more years than he could count on one hand. He simply had to smile a little on the surface but a whole big bunch from within. *This big kid was all right,* he thought, as he encourages the giant to grab his hat by saying, "Get your bonnet, son, and let's make like a bunch of Whooping Cranes and get the flock out of here."

"Yes, sir," Ernie retorted with a big old grin stretching across his mug. "Let's fly."

Ben opened the door, peeked out then let Ernie step out first but was quick to follow. When stepping from the door onto the veranda they together saw Rudy had Deputy Sheriff Barney occupied. Upon making eye contact, they knew instantly what they had to do when Rudy started acting like he was trying to scare away a bee. Throwing his hand from his ear in a motion that was signaling Ben and Ernie to get the lead out and get the heck out of sight. Making a scene like no coward you had ever seen, that was Rudy. Rudy knew with Ben and Ernie disappearing around the building corner, they had more likely than not reached the pickup. With the estimated time in check, Rudy became real agreeable with Barney thanking this sorry excuse for a cop for not locking him up. Then Rudy meandered down the street and Barney was really feeling like he finally had gotten the respect he deserved.

About three blocks away, Ben, driving his pickup, pulled up to the corner where Rudy was waiting, at which time, Rudy climbed in being a bit mystified as to the whereabouts of Ernie. Rudy, not being your average dummy, knew Ernie was there but couldn't quite grasp where that big tub of lard was hiding.

Ben turned left to drive right past the jailhouse and waved to Barney as they journeyed by without suspicion of their less-than-desirable action. Undesirable from a law man's point of view that is, a point of view that was without a doubt undeniably corrupt. Barney had grabbed a broom that had its resting place in the corner terrace near the door and was going through the motions of sweeping the sidewalk and gloating how he had shown that self-impressed, what was his name? Oh yeah, -Ben, that he would not mollycoddle anyone, not even a tough cowboy like him.

As they eased out of town, they witnessed in their rearview mirror Barney meticulously sweeping the porch to a finish and slowly moving to the sidewalk. Ben kept Barney in sight for a good distance but finally had to give up. Short in time, they wound to a stop near Rudy's truck and were wondering what it would take to get 'er running again.

Rudy couldn't stand himself any longer and blurted out, "Where's the big guy?" Ben started chuckling and said, "Okay, Ernie, you can come out now." Then the pickup started rocking when suddenly it seemed as though it was going to explode. Rudy got an uncharacteristic dumbfounded look across his plain but handsome features at the time of Ernie rising from beneath a tarp Ben has spread over him to keep him from sight. Failing to mention the fence posts and the rolls of barbed wire shouldn't be allowed for it simply added more to the natural appearance of what was seemingly happening. For that reason, was why the unaccustomed look of surprise from Rudy.

"Man, that was some idea, but you know, that would have crushed a normal man. You know what I'm driving at, all that weight. Jiminy Christmas! Twenty rolls of new barbed wire and those posts. That is a lot of weight," Rudy went on to say.

"Oh, heck, it was nothing!" Ernie assured. "No, nothing at all."

It seemed to be just that nothing at all as Ernie went about straightening out the disarray of wire and wood. By the time Ernie had straightened up the somewhat disarranged equipment a feeling of deja vu overcome him. A feeling he would face every now and again bringing back memories of South Dakota and riding the fence lines in the spring checking for broken wire or plainly downed fences. Remembering his boss and that he had to purchase a Morgan horse gelding that had the stature that included the strength and stamina that would sustain an all-day venture across some of the worst terrain in the badlands of this country: South Dakota. Ernie was not a fly-weight and that being a fact needed a real sturdy mount to carry him for 12 to 14 hours in the saddle.

"What's the problem, Ernie, you see a ghost?" Ben chided him good naturedly.

"Oh, no. I'm sorry," Ernie said. "Just thinking. Sorry."

Chapter Eleven

I N TIME PASSING THE WISE all-important Barney-by his own rul-
ing-was marveling at the efficient job he was doing or had done
grooming the porch which included the sidewalk and there about.
At this moment of marvel making a free-thinking pronouncement
which concluded that good help was hard to find. Help just wasn't
what it used to be. No, it sure as the devil was not.

Suddenly realization bombarded him with all the swift sureness
of the Japanese when calling to mind their initial bombing of Pearl
Harbor at the onset of World War II. Dropping like a ton of bricks,
heck he hadn't seen hide nor hair of Rosco. Perplexed and burdening
his mind he poked his head through the front door. Sort of gingerly like as if he was expecting an unwelcome challenge. "Rosco,
hey Rosco, you in here big buddy?" He questioned. The answer was
bold, the silence, so once again he posed the question with a little more urgency for he expected a certain response but once again
silence. A silence so bold that deafening is a telling description it is
having an informative and revealing rings. Barney trying to pacify an
urgency building told himself Rosco was probably in the can. Then
his mind wandering a bit thought how lucky they were that they
didn't have to use a can any longer and did have a big white porce-

lain commode. How lucky could he be, being employed by such an uptown municipality, he marveled at his good fortune.

Then he heard a snoring and figured it to be Ernie for at this time he hadn't any reason for a conjecture of difference. It was obnoxious and loud so decided he would have to wake ole fat so up.

Barney then developed heart and decided to do a good turn and let him sleep when out of nowhere there was a monstrous snoring sound which included a coughing and choking that would have rattled the dead. He couldn't stand it any longer and yelled. "Hey, Ernie, Ernie, wake up! I'm going to have to give you a ticket for excessive noise in a quiet zone." Still another snore then he yelled, louder this time, "Ernie, ERNIE, dang it, Ernie, wake up!" Then a "What, what is that, that you, Sheriff. This ain't Ernie, it's Rosco," he whined, "Sheriff, get me out of here would ya."

"Rosco, what in God's creation are you doing in there?" Barney wondered aloud! "Well Sheriff," Rosco came back with, "You wouldn't believe me if I told you, but this is what happened." Barney stopped him in his vocal tracks when he quite abruptly said. "Save it Rosco, save it for someone who wants to listen to your hogwash. I don't want any part of it. Where's Ernie, Rosco? You got an idea about that? You know F. F. is due back here any day or any time, what you have to say about that, Huh? How 'bout it, what you gotta say for yourself? Where's that big tub at?"

"Let me see," Rosco tried to make light of the situation. "I got a pretty good sleep." Then he smiled a crooked smile on a sheepish face, a face that only a mother could love including questioning eyes begging to be forgiven.

"How'd they get out of here without me spying them?" Barney asked. "Heck fire I was outside since early morning. What time was it when He got out and you got in?"

"Actually," Rosco said. He's only been gone for a couple of hours give or take a minute or two one way or the other. They left by the front door. They just walked out of here like they had nothing to hide. Just right out the door, they weren't being sneaky or nothing they just walked right out the door. By the way Barney where were you? You said you were outside all morning, what's was ya doing? Bet you were napping in your chair so you're trying to shame me playing make believe ain't cha? Huh, ain't cha, answer me, ain't cha. Shame, shame on you, Barney, shame, shame, shame, shame on you. Don't you know you can go to hell for telling a lie the same as you can for murder? You'd better straighten up Barney, yes sir you'd better repent. Yes, sir, you'd best be asking for forgiveness." Rosco had a spiel going and became proportionately hypnotized with his blame game and just couldn't bring himself to let well enough be.

"You're trying to put a lone gilt trip on me." Rosco implied. "Save it." Barney said, "I have an idea where they might be, come on let's see if I'm right, if we hurry, we may get there before it's too late. Barney opened the jailhouse door at which time Rosco stepped out stretched and remarked, "Sure is nice being a free man again." And again, stretched a big ole bear stretch at which time Barney said, "Don't you understand English I said we gotta put a hurry on. Let's GO! LIKE NOW NOT, TOMORROW!!" He recounted his orders in a fashion of urgency. As time would allow Rosco got the lead out and ultimately hurried to the black and white then bailed in the open door slamming it shut as he came to rest on a less than adequate seat.

Then Barney instructed him. "Buckle up!" Rosco did so reluctantly but upon completion said. "Done." Completion verified and Barney saying, "Hang on, Rosco." At which time Rosco braced himself by pushing against the dashboard. Barney turned the bubble gum lights on and goes unsaid the siren was a whaling its eardrum shattering screech. His final words were, "We gotta put a hurry on."

With his instructions complete, Barney started the black and white. He revved the engine a couple of times for effect then pushing the clutch in eased it into gear. Revved it a time or two more and let the clutch out suddenly with the car jumping ahead like it was jet propelled. Needless to say, they only went about five feet and were stopped abruptly. The power of the car kept them rolling but that in mind they hadn't any control for the steering was nonexistent. The cable that Rudy had strung under the car's carriage dislodged the two steering tires consequently it was spinning its tires riding on the front bumper and throwing sparks from hell to high water.

Rosco with a perplexed look spreading across his somber mug said, "Hey, Barney, there's something the matter with our squad car."

"No kiddin', Sherlock! What was your first clue, Dick Tracy?" Barney fumed back at him.

"I just thought you might ought to be told, you're always telling me-to tell you what I know so I'm telling ya and look where it gets me. See if I ever tell you anything again." Rosco pouted.

Barney tossed out a half fast apology to Rosco only to observe an effect that was minimal to none. In the while, he feebly attempted his ineffectual pardon me he was challenged by a wit from within not to feel remorse. Therefore, comfort for the day in and day out treatment that he deemed nothing short of abusive was not to be had, so poor, poor me, he sulked.

"Well my shrewd leader of unrelenting events what we going to do now." Rosco asked but didn't wait for Barney's answer and said, "Huh, what we going to do now, Boss Man?" Rosco had an unrelenting insistence which had the intention of receiving an answer that would satisfy his inquisitive but simple mind.

"Did ya hear me, Barney?" Rosco pressed looking for assurance that he had actually been heard.

"Yeah, Yeah, Yeah! How could I not hear your lips a-flapping, you big moron?" Barney threw back to him. "Just put a zipper on it, close your hole, Okay? Just shut up and let me think."

"Man, I just can't think of what to do. We ain't got anything to drive. What can we do?" Barney continued. Rosco was just sitting looking at Barney all so innocent but not answering the question directed to him. Rosco was just setting there and finally stuck his hand up not unlike a child in grade school wanting to get his or her teacher's attention.

"What are you doing?" Barney asked glaring at him.

"I, my fearless leader, have an idea and I didn't want to speak out of line so I raised my hand for permission to speak my mind. I didn't want to interrupt you and get my butt chewed out, don't ya know?" Rosco went on. "So be nice to me or I won't tell all!"

Chapter Twelve

In the meantime:

"You miss that Cowboy life, don't cha, Ernie?" Ben's curiously but gently probed with what was more a statement than a question.

"You could say that I reckon; it just sort of gets into a man's blood. That Strawberry Roan gelding, I really miss him. A heart that one had was just as big as the moon. I wonder who or if anyone is riding him. That is one horse that when the going got tough, he just sucked it up and got a-goin'. You just ain't ever seen anything like him," Ernie assured Ben.

"Well, Ernie, that's all well and good. I could go on talking horses all day, but first things first. We gotta get Rudy's truck a-runnin'," Ben reminded him.

"Yeah, that ain't gonna be a problem. The only thing we need to do is put some fuel in them blasted tanks. Then there's a hand pump on the side where the fuel pump is located. If it should prove that we have to bleed the fuel lines it will be much harder, but we won't find out standing around so let's hop to it."

Ernie tipped the hood over, so he was able to get next to the engine. While surveying his options, Rudy and Ben managed to pump fuel into the feeder tank. Once they had replaced the displaced fuel, Ernie started pumping the hand pump to prime the injectors. Luck at that moment seemed to be riding with Ernie when he told the friends he was more than sure that diesel was pumped up enough to try and start her.

Rudy jumped into the cab, inserted the key and said, "Here goes nothing!" As he turned the key, he pushed the start button and was momentarily sure that nothing was what was happening. The reward for trying to do the right thing seemed elusive as it spun over numerous times and gave the impression it was not going to start when suddenly a choking sound, a cough and that yellow engine started belching smoke in abundance. This was only short-lived and in a short time settled down to a rattling purr with the excess smoke gradually dissipating.

Rudy stepped out of the glorious Peterbilt smiling like a bloodhound with a mouth full of porcupine quills. His eyes were just a twinkling. Walking up to Ernie, he pounded him on the back enforcing his gratitude by saying, "Ernie, my man, you are worth your weight in gold, no doubt. Heck fire, your weight times five in gold is what you're worth."

The gratitude was accepted yet unexpected and for that reason Ernie was tongue-tied for a quick moment then finally got out, "Thank you, thank you, thank you very much, Rudy, it was nothing'. No, nothing at all. Glad it worked out."

"As I am, my man, whadda I owe you, Ernie?" Rudy asked with much sincerity.

"Good God, man, you've already paid me! Remember, you sprung me from Alcatraz or the likes of in my opinion. Mark it up as paid in full!" Ernie said with genuineness hanging on to each word making sure the proper emphasis would call attention to his statement "Paid in full!" when reiterating his feelings.

"Okay, okay, sorry I even asked!" Rudy managed to force out gulping for air between laughs. "I just didn't want you to think I didn't appreciate your expertise. I promise, I'll not mention it again. Case closed, end of story, that's all she wrote!"

"Hey, hey, you two quit your mutual love affair of admiration," Ben taunted, then followed with, "We've gotta figure out what'll we do next, I betcha one thing. I'll betcha a dollar to hole in a donut that good old Barney and Rosco haven't decide to go fishing, so we'd better get a move on, don't cha know." Ben sporting a quill smile.

Next, talk being short, the three cronies got their duffs in gear as they systematically picked up the tools and put them away.

"Let's go back to town," Rudy encouraged. "I'm gonna starve to death. Besides, I want to check out Peggy."

When hearing Rudy's words of reasoning, Ben couldn't help putting his two cents in when he said, "I knew it, Rudy, you just ain't gonna leave well enough alone, are ya? Women will be the ruination of you yet. Just get rid of one bitch and you're looking for another."

"Get off you high horse, Ben! You know when a man's hungry, he's hungry. Besides, look who's bumping his gums. The great one, who is only 80 pounds heavier than he ought to be," Rudy remarked and too included a substantial amount of body language when reminding Ben that he is the one who has said "I do" twice, not him. Being speechless was not a problem that offered much interference to Ben but he actually hadn't a comeback and only grunted his disgust of acknowledgement and said, "Let's head, let's do it."

All the time, Ernie was standing in the background listening to the two friends spout back and forth. When they had decided to venture back to the truck stop, Ernie started waving his hands back and forth, his arms being stretched in the air above his head.

Ben finally noticed Ernie and his silent motionless posturing then quizzed him. "What's your problem? Why were you waving your hands like that, big buddy?"

"It's like this. I was trying to get you guys' attention and you wouldn't hear me so I thought maybe if I waved my hands in the air you may give me my turn to talk and it worked." Ernie smiled.

Then together Ben and Rudy asked, "Well, whatcha want?"

Ernie then bluntly stated, "What about me, guys? Did ya forget about the pickle I'm in? What about me?"

"Ernie, you ride with me," Rudy said. "Jump in my sleeper and don't get out unless I tell ya to." Ernie said, "Okay!" and bailed into the truck and in one motion he would plunge headlong for the sleeper. You talk about rock, that air ride sleeper swayed back and forth giving the impression that it may just tip over, Rudy recalled. Later admitting he knew it wouldn't but still had an unwavering suspicion that his wary feeling just may become justified. With regards to his suspicion and time being brief, finally the sleeper settled. The thought dissipated for the rocking stopped. In that moment it loomed large in its Peterbilt splendor for it was only a pittance (a moment in time) that he was somewhat surprised, Rudy had said.

Rudy hollered, "Follow me, Ben." He fired his truck and sounded the six-inch straights!" Then he motioned with his arm to follow while sporting Ben's puppy dog smile.

Chapter Thirteen

S PINNING THAT OLD PETERBILT AROUND the parking area then onto the highway, he maneuvered. Rudy was playing, that implying he was toying with the musical sound of the exhaust system. Winding the engine's RPMs to a meager 2300 then letting off the throttle. The Jake brake then would bellow a gregarious guttural noise that was simply music to the ears of a seasoned or not-so- seasoned truck driver.

As Rudy straightened out his rig, he was pointing toward town. The rhythm and timing that was his with gaining speed while changing gears offered evidence of years of mastery behind the wheel of eighty-thousand pounds of deadly weaponry. Weaponry, only if this seventy-five-foot piece of equipment was not driven with the respect it so properly deserved.

The distance, not far, since beings a foot was a twist in the past. The fate of bad luck was only hours prior and not forgotten but stored in the backside of his mind. This would be a positive with respect to that.

Not having far to progress it wasn't necessary using each of the eighteen gears of forward motion at his disposal

Ernie was sitting on the rack gazing intently out the window when he raised his huge mitt, index finger extended, at the same time saying, "Hey, Rudy, look at what's a-comin'. Is that what it looks like?"

Rudy looking, then concluding, yes, it was! "You can bet your firstborn on it, Ernie. It darn sure is!"

Ernie muttered. "I was a-feared of that man. I gotta keep from sight. Them good for nothin' two-bit creeps."

A brainchild came to surface and as customary coming to mind from non-exacting instruction. With this the essence of thought pre-meditation, addressing this conundrum was nonexistent. Rudy intu-itively noticed Ben was not far behind so turned his Citizen Band radio on and at that time made what he hoped to be a successful holler at Ben by saying, "Hey, Gentle Ben, you got yer ears on?"

Then to Rudy's delight, an obnoxious voice on reply. "Yeah, yeah, yeah, ten-four, little buddy, they must be 'cause I can hear you loud and proud. What'cha want there, Silver Bullet? Copy?"

"Ten-four, I copy. You ain't gonna believe what's coming down the zipper in front of us. They're riding a two-seated bicycle, they being your two copper friends."

With that, Gentle Ben says, "Hey, Silver Bullet, have they reached the railroad crossing yet?"

"That is a negatory, Gentle Ben, they certainly have not. Say no more for I have a handle on the plan already!" The Bullet said, then instructed, "Ben, just fall back and let me do what needs to be done."

Wouldn't you know it, those two coppers representing some-one of being less than none for brain had stopped right in the middle of the train track. With that in tow, there may be a possibility of understanding such a calloused opinion. The setting couldn't have been more to the liking for as Rudy approached the crossing, he was slowly but systematically bringing his rig to a stop.

The policemen in regard were watching with wide eyes won-dering, trying to determine what was happening. That is when the funny part of this story took place. Rudy had installed an accessory air horn mounted on the frame between the sleeper and the front of his trailer. This horn wasn't the average air horn that big trucks are accustomed to having aboard when shipped from the factory. It was a special horn, one that sounded like a locomotive's blast of identification, one hundred percent the real deal. You can believe it or not but its bellow was as authentic as any train horn that the friends had ever heard, and if possible, probably a slight more genuine than the bona fide train horn.

So, the plan was just as Rudy was bringing his truck to a rest before the caution line, sooner than the tracks, he laid on that horn. You talk about two uniformed city cops jumping to race out of the way. Springing about a foot above the ground, and as if rehearsed, they turned one into the other once they had succeeded in getting their feet on the ground. This was reflexes in action and resulted in a collision knocking one another on the seats of their pants! They were frantic trying to get out of the way, for positive they were and beyond all doubt sure, they were about to become statistics run over by a train.

It was a comical sight witnessing them two scrambling for life, their life, they were sure. They managed to rise to their feet and still scurrying like cottontail rabbits running from a dog with an appetite. One of them grabbed the bicycle by the front wheel and tried to go one direction while the other had grabbed the back wheel trying to go the other way. Then continuing once again as if a skit and rehearsed they were pulling in opposite directions. As a result, they fell, both of them; the consequence of their actions was to land in prone positions another time.

Ben decelerated and unhurriedly brought his pickup to stop behind Rudy's semi-truck, rather "large car" as Rudy preferred. He at once removed himself from his aforementioned transportation and walked to where the commotion was in the undertaking. He then would raise one foot to the step below the tractor's driver door. Standing in that position while grasping the chrome hand hold mounted to the cab's side and saying with a look of disbelief, "Would you look at that? Would you just look at that! What a couple of morons. I gotta take that back, Rudy. Even a moron is smarter than that."

Ben stepped back as Rudy clambered out of his Pete. When getting to the ground he was laughing so hysterically it was dually the job keeping his foundation so double the work supporting himself.

"What the taxpayers pay in this day and age for is this?" Rudy choked. "Man, what a deal. The city ought to try and hire more fellers with such qualities as them two."

Rudy was simply being a smarty-pants but who could counter his statement of being incorrect or infallible? Ben surely wouldn't and there just was no one else in earshot to test the appropriateness of his opinion, so the story goes.

Then from the hub of two tangled bodies in disarray, came a bickering and name-calling contest that bears not a chance for replication. If such innuendos were heard by appropriate authorities, infecting the airwaves with such vulgarity would land a man (a person ... must be politically correct, so the ACLU doesn't get its tit in a ringer. Them morons can kiss my underside.) in the slammer!

Barney was screaming his head off at his subordinate saying "You fingdiot! Get your head outta yer a_ _. Watch where you're going damn it, just watch where you're a-going."

Rosco came back with a quick, "You talkin' to me?"

"Heck no, Rosco, I'm just a-yelling' at myself. You moron, who in the name of Christ would I be talking to besides you?" Barney regurgitated point blankly.

"Ahhh, I don't know. Who?" Rosco yelled in his flustered state of mind.

Ben and Rudy watched laughing quite unceremoniously and later concluded if there would have been onlookers to perceive sound, they would have heard nose snorts only this time coming from them two. The sound similarity was an echo that was not unlike the noise that erupted from the clandestine witch that Rudy had spoken with earlier. A call referring to his dilemma and was an innocent call that should have initiated the start of its resolve. A phone call that stated misfortune and asking for assistance in rectifying this bit of bad luck.

Hardly able to get his question presented from lack of oxygen resulting from uncontrollable laughter, Ben posed to Rudy, "Don't you suppose we should get going and let these clowns hash it out by their lonesome?"

Rudy came back with a quick reply saying, "Yep, sounds like a plan to me. Let's ride."

With that rejoinder, Ben hustled to his pickup, crawled into and simultaneously Rudy clambered aboard his Pete. Firing her up, releasing the air brakes, dropping it into low gear, engaging the clutch and as he started rolling, arm whirling like the propeller on an airplane motioning for Ben to follow. He did all of this with timing that was natural, thus giving an impression that all had been rehearsed. You may judge it to be such for he had done this so many times it was quite natural for him; it wasn't even necessary giving his actions a second thought, for this he had done this many times previously so by and large it had become usual and using no more concentration collectively than breathing.

His Pete rolling, Rudy continued watching Barney and Rosco in his rearview mirror. It would have been great to have a video camera as this no doubt would have been the funniest of funnies for America's Funniest Videos.

Then suddenly, Ben flying around Rudy's truck, while hollering something on the radio about the last one to the truck stop would have to buy dinner and beer for the evening.

Rudy started a-shaking his head thinking' his old pal hadn't changed an iota.

Chapter Fourteen

T HAT BELLOW, IT RATTLED THE sturdiest of windows. A noise unparalleled and not unlike a pair locomotives meeting while simultaneously proceeding in a fashion of full speed, separate directions naturally, with horns just a-blasting. The fat man, F. F. Fichen, was uncomfortable and that being the case was doing everything in his power to make anyone who was anybody aware of his discomfort.

Truth be told, experiencing physical pain was actually minimal while comparing such to the intellectual torment that had taken a toll on his mental stature. He had never been whipped on so severely in his entire life. The fact of the matter is, he'd never been beaten when instigating or responding to a foul-mouthed barbaric action of fisticuffs in his life's entirety. For F. F. admitted it was unnerving and his embarrassment in addition was beyond comprehension so needless to say the happening that was left in the balance gave an impression to Mr. Fichen as being vastly unfair and had not held a choice or if you'd rather, options!

In various fashions came threats of bodily harm. Inclusive of these suggestions where to put instruments in a place that wouldn't benefit a soul if so implanted! He was really out of sorts, and he never having been in an emergency room from the standpoint we speak of actually makes it somewhat understandable. With regards to his verbal shenanigans, the in-your-face innuendos were in real-time, the percussion of his voice nearly crushing.

The reason for good old F. F being somewhat disposed may give way to others in reference to manners ... and lack thereof. End result getting a whipping put on him like he had never known! He would probably never be inconvenienced at another time in the manner of such a violent trouncing that finished in such humiliation.

You see, Fearless Floyd, having an overbearing personality which is and was his downfall, had driven up on a pickup and horse trailer meandering slowly and seeming to be headed nowhere real fast.

Blaring was F. F.'s horn, sounding a piercing noise as well as escorting his personality, impatient as usual, and this episode of blatant misconduct seemed to be nothing unlike his every day protocol. His three hundred pounds of fat that sported long shaggy hair and grizzly whiskers. A prime setting to house such an overbearing conduct.

His car was a big old what-cha-call it and the brightest color of pink you could ever imagine. Good Old F. F. really thought he was the cat's meow.

He continued honking and finally the pickup and horse trailer started a time-consuming pause moving slower than ever and finally stopped dead in its tracks. The door swung open and out stepped BEN and by now you know where this story is headed.

Ben looked around without a care and ever so slowly walked back to F. F.'s effervescent automobile. Stretching like big old grizzly bear that had just emerged from hibernation, he sidled up to F. F.'s ride ever so cool and propelling one arm back behind him then the other trying to loosen his muscles because when riding a fair distance in his pickup he got quite stiff. When getting next to the gypsy wagon or whatever you choose to call the pink cruiser, he issued an order to Mr. Fat Man. In no uncertain terms and far from being pleasant he exhaled a demand of, "Remove your overbearing fat ass from your pimp-mobile. Just so procrastination is not a problem, that means now, and I mean like right now or sooner, please!" Ben finished his directive with mocking politeness.

By this time, the indignant, pompous F. F. was getting rather put out and was inclined to believe what he had predisposed as to what was going to happen. You see, no one spoke to him with such disrespect. But then there was Ben. Tune in to the next book to find out about the do's and don'ts with Ben in the picture! Hmmm!

www.ingramcontent.com/pod-product-compliance
Lightning Source LLC
Chambersburg PA
CBHW031034190726
48286CB00003BA/1177